So That's How They Sleep

By Rishi Oberoi

So That's How They Sleep

North's Adventures

It was all over the news.
Something strange was happening at the zoo.

But what?

The zoo was loud with cries and squeaks.
Oh no, the baby animals were not sleeping!

No one knew what to do.

In a house not so far away,
little North was listening.

"Is there a way to help
those babies sleep?"

No one knew this secret, but
North could speak to animals
and knew just what to do.
So off North went to the zoo.

First came...

The moody monkeys and their infants.
Out of control, the infants were howling and squeaking.

"Why are you making so much noise?"
North asked in a sweet voice.
"We are so very tired," said the infants.
Smiling, North hummed a melody,
then began to sing.

Rock-a-bye baby, on the tree top.
When the wind blows, the cradle will rock.
When the bough breaks, the cradle will fall.
And down will come baby, cradle and all.

One by one, the infants nodded off to sleep.
And then came...

The zesty zebras and their twin foals, who weren't getting along.
One was black with white stripes.
The other was white with black stripes.

"Why are you two fighting?" asked North.
"We can't sleep. We are scared," said the twins.
So North began to sing.

Twinkle, twinkle, little star,
how I wonder what you are!
Up above the world so high,
like a diamond in the sky.

When the blazing sun is gone,
when he nothing shines upon,
then you show your little light,
twinkle, twinkle, all the night.

Then the traveler in the dark,
thanks you for your tiny spark.
He could not see which way to go,
if you did not twinkle so.

In the dark blue sky, you keep,
often through my curtains peep.
For you never shut your eye,
till the sun is in the sky.

'Tis your bright and tiny spark,
lights the traveler in the dark.
Tho' I know not what you are,
twinkle, twinkle, little star.

Just like that, the foals
were fast asleep.
And then came...

The graceful giraffes and their sad-looking calves.
"Why are you feeling sad?" North asked.

"We are tired but cannot sleep.
Tell us how you fall asleep, North."
North smiled and began to sing.

Hush, little baby, don't say a word;
Mama's gonna buy you a mockingbird.
And if that mockingbird don't sing,
Mama's gonna buy you a diamond ring.
And if that diamond ring turns brass, Mama's
gonna buy you a looking glass.
And if that looking glass gets broke,
Mama's gonna buy you a billy goat.
And if that billy goat doesn't pull,
Mama's gonna buy you a cart and bull.
And if that cart and bull turn over,
Mama's gonna buy you a dog named Rover.
And if that dog named Rover won't bark,
Mama's gonna buy you a horse and cart.
And if that horse and cart fall down, well,
you'll still be the sweetest baby in town.

Just like that, one by one, the
calves nodded off.
And then came...

The stellar seals and their pups.
The pups stared at North as if talking with their big dark eyes.
"Don't you fret, let me sing you a song to help you sleep," said
North, who began to sing.

Row, row, row your boat,
gently down the stream.
Merrily, merrily, merrily, merrily,
life is but a dream.
Row, row, row your boat,
gently down the stream.
Merrily, merrily, merrily, merrily,
life is but a dream.

Row, row, row your boat,
gently down the stream.
Merrily, merrily, merrily,
merrily,
life is but a dream.

*Just like that, the pups
drifted off to sleep.
And then came...*

The elegant elephant and its calf.

"Oh, North, can you help my baby sleep?" asked the elephant. North knew just the lullaby to help mommy and baby elephant and began to sing.

Lullaby and goodnight, with roses bestride.
With lilies bedecked beneath baby's sweet bed.
May thou sleep, may thou rest, may thy slumber be blest.
May thou sleep, may thou rest, may thy slumber be blest.

Just like that, the calf rolled over to sleep.
And then came...

The beastly bears with their cubs.
The cubs were huffing and chomping, growling and barking.

"Oh, please help us sleep. We are so tired," cried the bears.
North hurried to calm them down and began to sing.

Come, let's to bed, says Sleepy-head,
Tarry a while, says Slow,
Put on the pan, says Greedy Nan,
Let's sup before we go.

Just like that, the cubs cuddled together
and rocked themselves to sleep.
And then came...

The perky penguins and their chicks.
Slipping everywhere because they were tired and sleepy.
"Where is my brother?" asked one chick.
"Where is my sister?" asked another.

"Now come gather together around, and I'll help you sleep," said North, who began to sing.

Little boy blue, come blow your horn.
The sheep's in the meadow; the cow's in the corn.
Where is the little boy who looks after the sheep?
He's under the haystack, fast asleep.

*Just like that, the chicks swaddled
next to each other and shut their eyes.
And finally, it was time for...*

The legendary lions and their cubs.
So loud and roaring, they scared everyone away.
Everyone but North, who knew just what to do.
"I have your favorite song to help you sleep,"
said North, who began to sing.

Sleep, my love, and peace attend thee,
all through the night.
Guardian angels, God will send thee,
all through the night.
Soft, the drowsy hours are creeping,
hill and vale in slumber sleeping.
In my loving vigil keeping,
all through the night.

While the moon her watch is keeping,
all through the night.
While the weary world is sleeping,
all through the night.
O'er thy spirit gently stealing,
visions of delight revealing.
Breathes a pure and holy feeling,
all through the night.

And just like that,
the cubs all gave a
big yawn and went
to sleep.

23

One by one, all the baby animals went to sleep.
One by one, all the mama and papa animals went to sleep.
One by one, all the zookeepers, the doctors,
and the visitors went to sleep.

Caution!
Colder Zone

Until there was no one left awake.

Except...

One little child...

Made in the USA
Las Vegas, NV
15 December 2024

14286686R10017